Find a Cow NOW!

by Janet Stevens and
Susan Stevens Crummel

Holiday House / New York

HOLIDAY HOUSE is registered in the U.S. Patent and Trademark Office.
Printed and Bound in July 2012 at Kwong Fat Offset Printing Co., Ltd.,
Dongguan City, China.
The text typeface Allise.
The illustrations were done in acrylic paints, pencil, and collage.
www.holidayhouse.com
First Edition
1 3 5 7 9 10 8 6 4 2

Library of Congress Cataloging-in-Publication Data
Stevens, Janet.
Find a cow now! / Janet Stevens and Susan Stevens Crummel. — 1st ed.
p. cm.
Summary: Tired of hearing Dog yipping at chairs and trying to round up rugs,
Bird tells him to go to the country to find a cow, but this is one cattle dog
who does not know a cow when he sees one.
ISBN 978-0-8234-2218-0 (hardcover)
[1. Dogs—Fiction. 2. Domestic animals—Fiction.
3. Cows—Fiction. 4. City and town life—Fiction.]
I. Crummel, Susan Stevens. II. Title.
PZ7.S84453Fin 2012
[E]—dc23
2011042112

*For Blake, who herded us in the right direction,
and for Houdini, the silly cattle dog
who still needs a cow NOW!
—J. S. and S. S. C.*

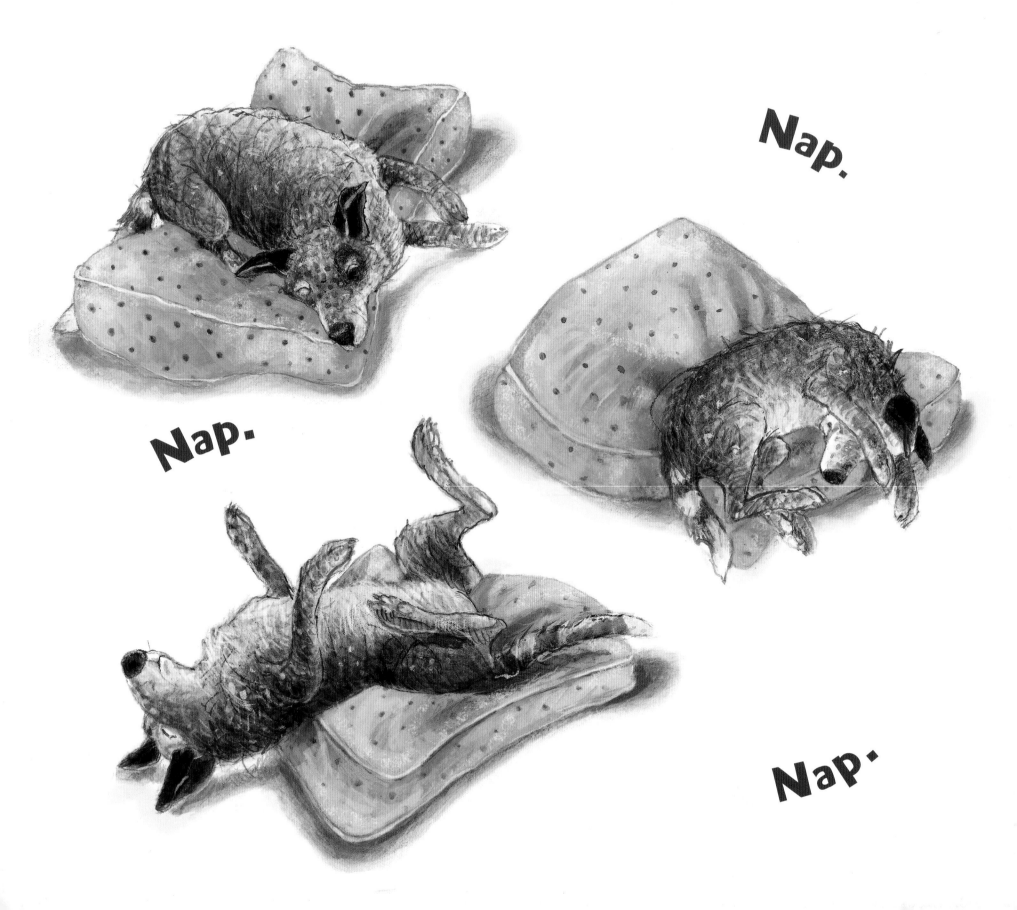

Nap.

Nap.

Nap.

Nap.

Dog was tired of naps.

He needed to chase. **Ruff! Ruff!**

He needed to move. **Yip! Yip!**

He needed to round up.

Yee-haw!

"STOP IT!" screeched Bird.

"You're driving me crazy, silly cattle dog. You're supposed to herd cows. Not chairs, not rugs. You need a cow."

"What's a cow?" asked Dog.

"I don't know," replied Bird. "But a cow is not in the city. A cow must be out there in the country. Go! Find a cow NOW!"

"Okay, Bird. I'll go to the country—
to find me a cow."

Dog rode down the elevator.
Nobody noticed.

Dog walked through the streets.
Nobody noticed.

Dog walked and walked until city turned to country.
There it was. . . .

CLUCK CLUCK!

PECK PECK!

"I am NOT a cow, silly dog.
I'm a CHICKEN! Leave me alone!"

Dog walked and walked. There it was. . . .

"A COW!"

Ruff! Ruff!

Yip! Yip!

Yee-haw!

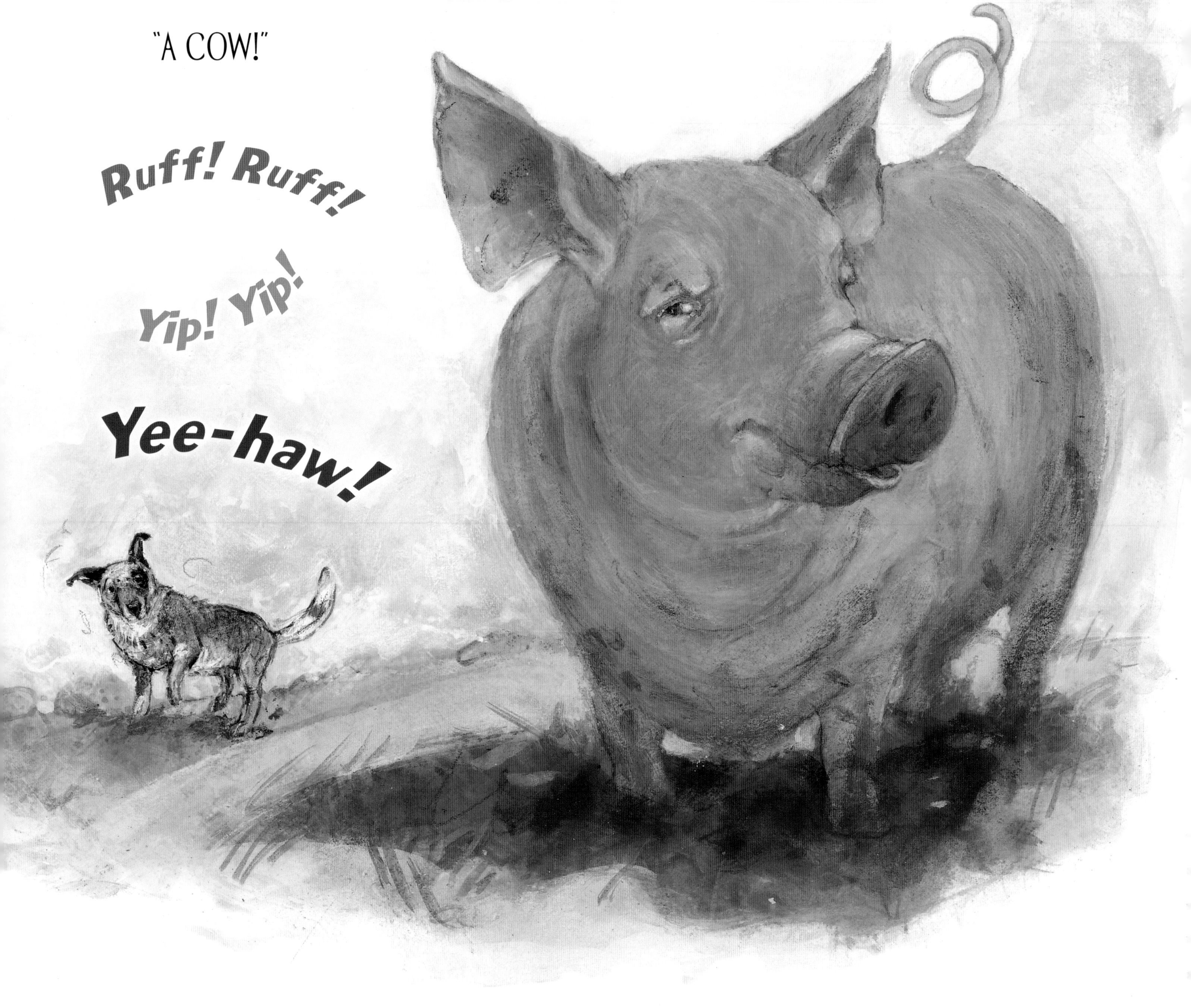

"I am NOT a cow, silly dog.
I'm a PIG! Leave me alone!"

OINK OINK!

SNORT!
SNORT!

Dog walked and walked.
There it was. . . .

"I am NOT a cow, silly dog.
I'm a DONKEY! Leave me alone!"

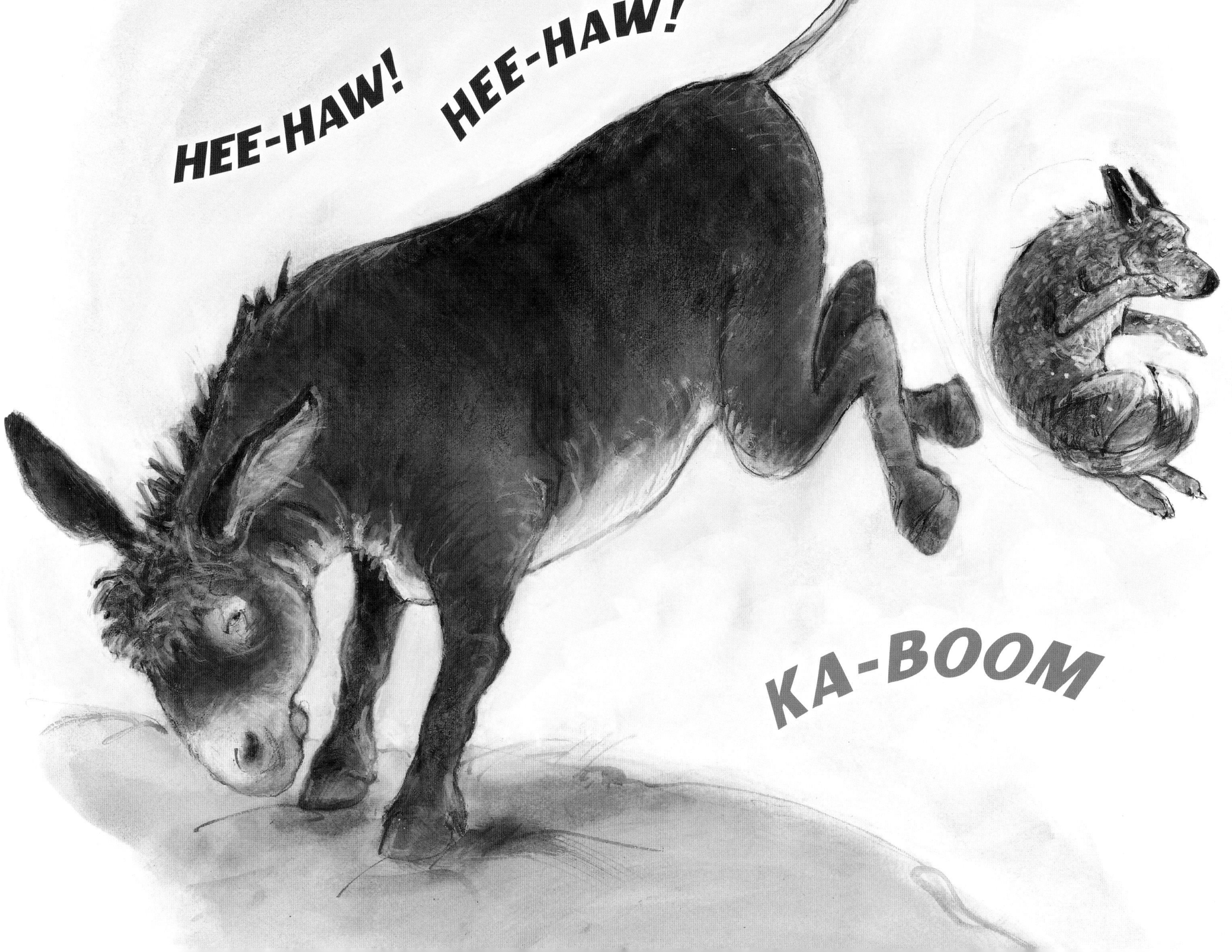

"Are you okay?"
"No."
"Need some help?"
"I want to go home."

They walked and walked until country turned to city.

They walked through the streets
of the city. Nobody noticed.
But then . . .

"What's going on?"

"Good grief!"

"Is that a . . ."

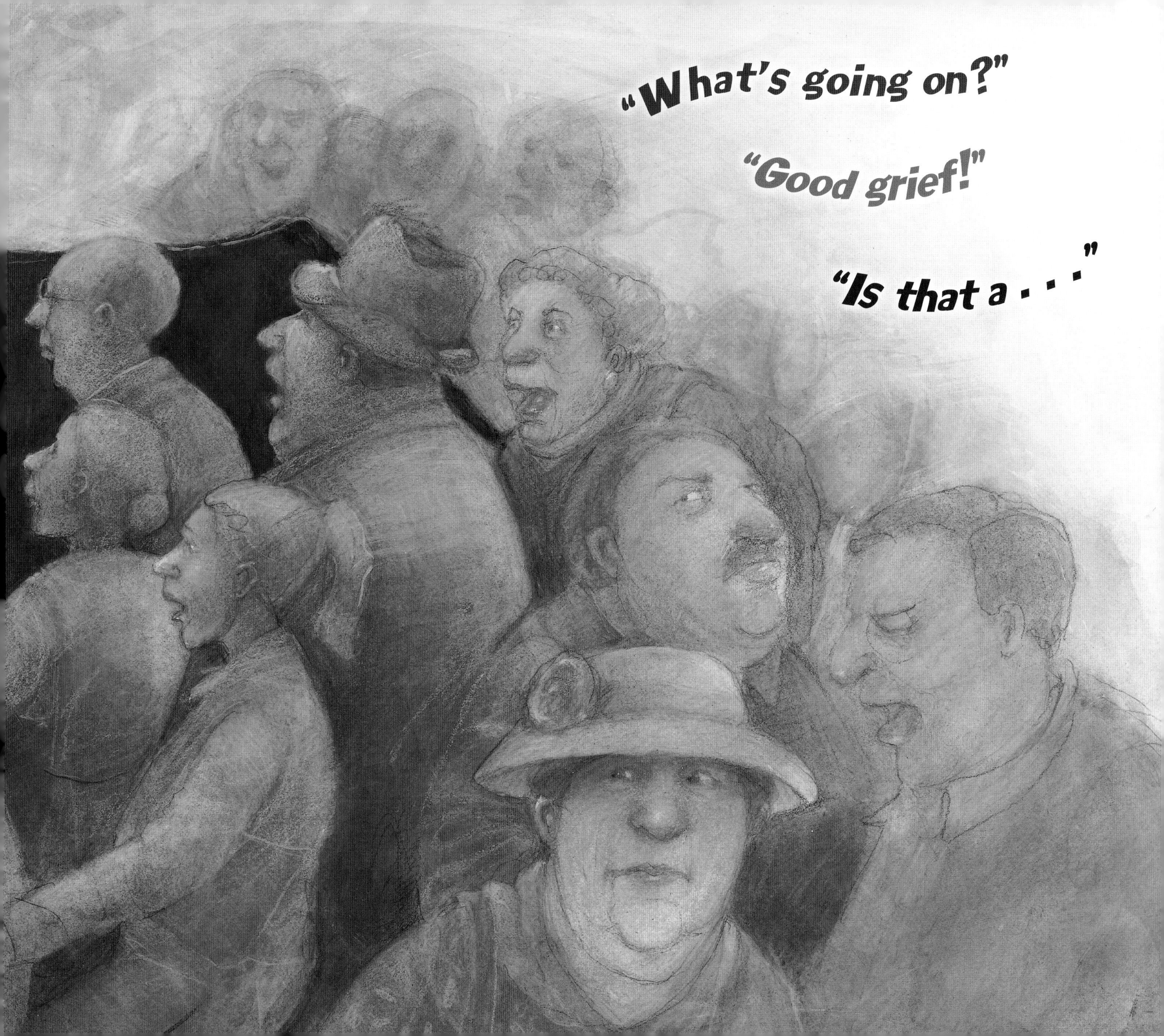

"Are you okay?"
"Yeah."
"My name is Dog. What's yours?"

"Can you stay?"
"It's late. Time to go home.
But I'll be back."
"Thanks, Dog."
"Thanks, Cow."

"Bird, I'm home."
   "Did you find a cow?"
"Yeah."
   "Did you herd it?"
"Oh, yeah."
   "You did? Was it fun?
   What did it look like?
   Was it big? Did you . . ."
"Stop it, silly bird.
I'm tired.
I need a nap."